5-MINUTE STORIES

HARPER

An Imprint of HarperCollinsPublishers

Fancy Nancy: 5-Minute Stories

"Chez Nancy" adapted by Nancy Parent. Based on the episode by Krista Tucker. "Nancy's Dog Show Disaster" adapted by Krista Tucker. Based on the episode by Matt Hoverman. "Camp Fancy" adapted by Laurie Israel. Based on the episode by Andy Guerdat. "Nancy Makes Her Mark" adapted by Nancy Parent. Based on the episode by Matt Hoverman. "School de Fancy" adapted by Nancy Parent. Based on the episode by Laurie Israel. "Nancy's Ghostly Halloween" adapted by Krista Tucker. Based on the episode by Laurie Israel. "Toodle-oo, Miss Moo" adapted by Victoria Saxon. Based on the episode by Laurie Israel. "Nancy Goes to Work" adapted by Krista Tucker. Based on the episode by Andy Guerdat. "Shoe La La!" adapted by Victoria Saxon. Based on the episode by Laurie Israel. "The Case of the Disappearing Doll" adapted by Nancy Parent. Based on the episode by Laurie Israel. "Mademoiselle Mom" adapted by Nancy Parent. Based on the episode by Sarah Katin and Nakia Trower Shuman. "Ice Skater Extraordinaire" adapted by Krista Tucker. Based on the episode by Krista Tucker.

All stories illustrated by the Disney Storybook Art Team.

Table of Contents

Chez Nancy 5

Nancy's Dog Show Disaster 21

Camp Fancy 37

Nancy Makes Her Mark...................................53

School de Fancy...69

Nancy's Ghostly Halloween.............................85

Toodle-oo, Miss Moo......................................99

Nancy Goes to Work.....................................115

Shoe La La! 131

The Case of the Disappearing Doll..................147

Mademoiselle Mom.......................................163

Ice Skater Extraordinaire..............................179

Chez Nancy

I have a new playhouse! My best friend, Bree, and I are planning a party to celebrate. I can't wait for my dad and grandpa to finish building it in our backyard.

Bree and I even made these fancy invitations to my playhouse-warming party. Aren't they *fantastique?* That's French for fantastic!

After Bree and I deliver the invitations to our friends, we see Grace riding up to us.

"Have you guys seen my new bike?" she asks. "I just got it."

"It's great!" Bree says.

Then Grace sees one of the playhouse-warming invitations.

"I've had a playhouse since I was little," she says. "Mine has a swing and a slide."

"Well my playhouse is more Lavish," I say. That's a fancy word for fancy.

"It has a fountain and butterfly doors."

"No, it doesn't," says Grace.

"Oui, yes, it does," I say. "It's more like a play palace. Come at three and see for yourself."

"I will!" she says, and rides away on her bike.

Bree and I go home to see if my playhouse is done yet.

Dad and Grandpa are picking up tools when we walk into the backyard.

"Just in time, girls," Dad says. "We're finished."

"Oh, Merci, Dad and Grandpa," I say. That's French for thank you. I'm excited to see my playhouse at last!

Bree and I look at the playhouse.

I'm confused. "This is not fancy," I say. "What about my butterfly doors and my fountain?"

"Maybe it's better on the inside," says Bree.

We go inside, and it's not better. It's not at all like I imagined.

"This is not fancy," I say.

I can't let Grace see this after I said how fancy my play palace was going to be!

Suddenly, I have an idea.

"We'll just have to turn it into a play palace ourselves!" I say.
"We'll make it fancy."

I ask my little sister, JoJo, and her friend Freddy for help. We hurry
and scurry. We fix and fluff.

JoJo and Freddy give us the sail from their pirate ship to make a butterfly door. We use Christmas lights to make a chandelier. That's fancy for a hanging light.

JoJo and Freddy make a fountain by the front door. Voilà! Fancy! My playhouse is ready.

As soon as we finish, our friends start to arrive.

"Bonjour, everyone," I say. "Welcome to my play palace."

"Wow, Nancy!" says Wanda.

"This is amazing!" agrees Rhonda.

"Merci," I say.

"It really is a play palace," says Wanda.

"I told you it was fancy," I say.

Grace looks all around. She doesn't say a word.

JoJo and Freddy come inside the playhouse and head straight for the snacks table.

"Yeah! Snacks!" they say. Grace smiles and puts her hand on her hip.

"I suppose your playhouse would be fancy if you didn't have to share it with them," says Grace, looking over to my little sister and her friend. "I get my playhouse to myself because it's all mine."

Maybe Grace is right. Sometimes JoJo and Freddy can be annoying.

"My playhouse is for big kids only," I tell JoJo.

"No, we wanna stay," she says.

"Yeah! Why can't we stay?" asks Freddy.

JoJo looks really sad. I smile at her. "I need you to go back to your ship and protect the play palace from pirates! Okay?"

"Now that they're gone, this place is perfect," says Grace. "I love it so much that I'll be coming over to play all the time."

"All the time?" I say.

"Yes," says Grace. "We should make a sign that says, Big Kids Only."

This feels all wrong! JoJo and Freddy helped when I needed them. They just wanted to play with us. I never should have kicked them out. They can't help that they're little!

"I'm going outside to apologize," I tell Bree.

I tell JoJo and Freddy I changed my mind. "Everyone is welcome!" I say. "I'm sorry. We can share the playhouse. Come by anytime you want."

"Really?" JoJo says.

"Mais oui, of course," I say.

JoJo and Freddy come back. I hope Grace will stay and play with everyone, but she wants to go.

"You can visit anytime, Grace," I say. "But the pirates might be here too."

I go back to the party with JoJo and Freddy. I look around at all my friends having fun together.

"I'd like to make a toast," I say. That's a fancy thing people do when they want to say something nice about someone.

"Here's to JoJo, Freddy, and Bree, who helped make my playhouse fancy." I say. "I have the best playhouse and friends ever!"

Nancy's Dog Show Disaster

Bree and I are watching a dog show on TV. Dog shows are *très elegant*. Dogs do tricks and then a judge decides which dog is best. That lucky dog wins a trophy.

That's when I get an idea. We should have a dog show in my backyard!

"I'll spread the word!" says Bree. "Then I'll get Waffles so we can practice."

Bree arrives with her dog, Waffles. Since I'm practically an expert at dog shows, I explain how it's done.

"First the dogs need to show that they're obedient," I say. That's fancy for they do what you say.

Bree tells Waffles to sit and lie down. Waffles does everything Bree says. "Good dog, Waffles!" says Bree.

"Now Frenchy will demonstrate the fancy part of the contest, when dogs show off their special skills," I say.

I know Frenchy is going to be more than good. He's going to be spectacular!

I hold up a hoop and say, "Jump, Frenchy!"

But Frenchy doesn't jump. Instead, he barks and runs away!

"Stop, Frenchy!" I shout.

He runs toward Mrs. Devine and her little dog, Jewel. Frenchy wants to play! But Jewel does not want to play.

"It's okay, Jewel," Mrs. Devine says. "Leap."

Jewel jumps right into her arms. I grab Frenchy's collar, feeling embarrassed that he didn't listen to my commands. I tell Bree that Frenchy's had enough practice for now.

"Okay," says Bree. "See you at the dog show!"

I practice with Frenchy in private.

"If you want to win, you must be obedient," I tell him.

Then I see Frenchy looking at my hoop. Now I understand! Frenchy doesn't want to do those boring moves. He wants to do a fancy trick!

I hold up the hoop and say, "Frenchy, *jeté!*" That's French for leap.

But Frenchy doesn't jeté. Instead, he gives me doggy kisses.

"Oh, Frenchy, I adore you too," I say. "But doggy kisses won't win us the dog show!"

Just then, the other contestants arrive.

"Let's do this!" says Lionel. He has brought his dog, Flash.

"Yeah! Waffles can't wait!" says Bree.

Rhonda and Wanda will be the judges. They even brought a trophy for the winners. They go over the rules.

"To get this trophy, a dog must be obedient and show off their special skill," Rhonda explains.

"I just don't understand . . . " I tell Frenchy. "Since
I'm fancy, my dog should be fancy too."

I am practically pouring my heart out to Frenchy, but instead
of listening to me, he runs after Jewel again!

"Come back!" I shout.

Mrs. Devine sees Frenchy coming and says, "Jewel, leap!"
Again, Jewel leaps right into her arms!

Jewel is très fancy. If I had a dog like her, I'd win the dog show
absolument. That's French for absolutely! That gives me a brilliant
idea! I ask Mrs. Devine if she will do me a favor.

"Of course!" says Mrs. Devine. "Anything for you, Nancy!"

The dog show is ready to begin!

"Where's Frenchy?" Bree asks. I explain that Frenchy is
indisposed. That's fancy for he can't make it. Luckily, Jewel can take
his place.

"No fair!" says Lionel. "I've seen Jewel do fancy tricks."

But Rhonda and Wanda say it's okay. A dog's a dog, so I can
compete with Jewel!

We start with part one, obedience We tell our dogs to sit, stand, and lie down.

All the dogs do what we say. But Jewel is by far the most elegant.

32

Halfway through the competition, Rhonda and Wanda announce that Jewel and I are in the lead!

"Magnifique! We're winning!" I tell Jewel. "Do you want to give me doggy kisses to celebrate?"

But Jewel turns away, uninterested. She doesn't even want to cuddle!

Rhonda and Wanda say that now it's time for the dogs to show off their special skills.

Waffles does a backflip. "Yeah! Good boy, Waffles!" says Bree.

Flash catches a disc in the air. "Nice one, Flash!" shouts Lionel.

Now it's time for Jewel to show off her special skill. I'm almost one hundred percent positive that once the judges see Jewel leap through the hoop, we'll win that trophy!

I hold up the hoop for Jewel.

But then I see Frenchy in the window. He looks really sad.

I begin to miss Frenchy terribly. Oh, there's not a word fancy enough to describe how much I love him!

"Frenchy! Here, boy!" I shout.

Frenchy is so excited, he runs out of the doggy door.

Wanda blows her whistle. "Nancy, you can't show two dogs!" she says. "You're disqualified!"

"Bree and Waffles win the dog show!" says Rhonda.

"I don't care if we didn't win," I tell Frenchy. "To me, you're still the best dog in the world!"

Frenchy just barks. I think that's dog for happy.

Camp Fancy

Usually I adore Saturdays but today I am très bored. I help Dad clean out the garage and soon find an old tent. Dad says he and Mom used to go camping all the time. A camping trip sounds spectacular!

"Can we go camping now?" I ask Dad.

"There may be a campsite close by . . ." Dad says.

"How parfait!" I say. That's French for perfect.

Dad leads me to the campsite . . . our backyard!

"B-but aren't we going camping in the wilderness?" I ask.

"We'll still have a blast," Dad says. "Besides, one of the first rules of camping is to make the best of what you have. Now come on, camper!"

Dad is right. I'm one hundred percent positive we can make this camping trip extra fancy!

Mom and JoJo are excited about our backyard campout. We get to work setting up the campsite.

I help Dad put up the tent, but it's trés difficile! That's French for very hard.

Finally, the tent is up.

"Great work, Nancy," Dad says. "Now let's light the campfire.
We can make s'mores!"

Mom goes to light the campfire when ping! ting! It starts to rain!

JoJo giggles as she uses one of the cups to catch the raindrops.

"No, JoJo!" I say. "This isn't good. Everything is getting soaking wet!"

"It's okay, Nancy," Dad says. "Now come on, everyone, into the tent!

"Make room, girls," Mom says as we crowd inside.

Dad turns on the lantern and the tent illuminates. That's fancy for lights up.

"Sacrebleu! Oh no!" I say. "Our campout is more than wrecked, it's ruined!"

"Hey, a little rain won't stop us from having fun," Dad says. "Let's just make the best of it!"

Dad starts to make shadow puppets using our lantern. He makes a bunny with his two fingers.

"Oh, I've got one," I say.

I use my hands to make a papillon. That's French for butterfly.

"See?" Dad says, "A little rain can't stop our campout!"

But then, splat! A raindrop hits my nose! Then another!
And another!

"Oh, beans," Dad says. "The tent is leaking. Let me see what
I can do."

Dad tries to fix the leak, but the entire tent falls down!

"Let's make the best of it . . . in the house," Dad says. We race
out of the tent for home.

We dry off inside, but I can't help feeling upset.

"No stars. No campfire. No tent. Our campout is a *fiasco!*" I say. That's fancy for everything has gone wrong.

Mom takes out some marshmallows. "We can still have s'mores!" she says.

But the wind howls. The lights flicker. Then they shut off completely. Blackout!

"The storm knocked out the power," Mom explains. "But at least we're safe inside."

Plip!. . .Plip! Ploop!

Water is dripping from the ceiling! "The roof sprung a leak too," Dad sighs. JoJo and I hold the flashlights as Mom and Dad set out pots to catch the water.

I feel really bad for Dad. "He just wanted everyone to have fun,"
I tell JoJo. Then I see Dad's shadow on the wall and get an idea.
"I know how we can save this campout!"

A little later, I call from the den. "Mom! Dad! Come to our campout, s'il vous plaît!" That's French for please.

"Aw, Nancy," I hear Dad say. "I'm afraid the campout's over."

But Mom and Dad freeze when they see how JoJo and I turned the den into a campsite extraordinaire. We set out a green towel for grass and hung a blanket over the couch for a tent.

"There's even a campfire!" Mom gushes as she admires pieces of orange paper in the campfire pit we made.

"Time for stargazing, everyone!" I call out.

Everyone sits around the campfire. I tell them to turn off their flashlights. Then I put a spaghetti strainer on top of Dad's lantern. Now there are tons of little white dots on the ceiling.

"Ta-da! Our very own Milky Way!" I shout.

"Amazing!" Dad says. Everyone looks up at the ceiling. The stars have everyone MeSMerized. That's fancy for when you can't take your eyes off something.

"I see the Big Dipper!" says JoJo.

Then I hand out marshmallows, chocolate, and graham crackers. Everyone makes s'mores.

"Bon appétit!" I say.

Then the lights flick on. The power is back!

"Awww!" we all say.

Dad smiles and turns the lights back off. Our campout continues!

We all munch on s'mores and continue to gaze at the stars.

Dad says, "I'm proud of you, Nancy-pants. You really made the best of it."

Nancy Makes Her Mark

Today, Dad has big plans. He's going to fix the Grand Canyon. That's what we named the giant crack in our front walkway.

"It's a surprise for Mom!" he says. "I just need the right supplies." Dad pulls a bucket, shovel, and big bag of cement out of the garage.

"All I need to do is pour this cement," he says.

"Cement?" I say. "How fancy!"

My best friend, Bree, gives me a funny look. "Cement is fancy?" she asks.

"It can be! Look at my pictures," I say to Bree. "Aren't they fabulous?"

"Movie stars put their handprints in cement for people to come and see. It makes them MeMorable!" That's fancy for being famous forever.

"So since your dad is making cement . . ." Bree says.

"We're going to put our handprints in it!" I say.

I ask Dad for permission to put our handprints in the wet cement.

"It will give the walkway pizzazz!" I say. That's fancy for style.

"Please, Mr. Clancy!" says Bree.

"Mom will love it!" I say.

"You know, Nancy, I think she would," says Dad. "Mom would love to see JoJo's handprints too."

JoJo and Bree make their
handprints. Then it's my turn.

"Now we will be famous
forever," I say.

JoJo gets cement on her
overalls, so Dad takes her inside
to clean up.

I look down at my work.
Hmm . . . Something is
missing . . .

I know what's missing! The movie stars didn't just leave handprints. They left footprints too.

"I'm almost one hundred percent positive that leaving footprints will make me even more memorable!" I say. "I think I'm going to need your help, Bree."

Bree uses my boa to help me balance. I put my shoes on my hands and leave footprints in the wet cement.

"My prints are parfait," I say. That's French for perfect. Except…

"They're still not very fancy," I say.

"But how can we make our prints fancy?" asks Bree. "It's not like cement comes in glitter!"

THAT'S IT!

We'll sprinkle glitter on our prints while the cement is still wet!

"I'll get the glitter!" Bree says.

But when Bree goes inside, my dog, Frenchy, gets loose!

"Frenchy! No! The walkway is still wet!" I shout. But Frenchy won't stop.

"Bree, you get the glitter," I say. "I'll get Frenchy!"

I run to keep Frenchy away from the wet cement. "Frenchy! Stop, s'il vous plaît!" That's French for please.

Frenchy chases after a squirrel. I chase after Frenchy.

"Frenchy, no!" I yell.

When Frenchy chases the squirrel up a tree, he accidentally bumps into me and sends me spinning. I trip over my boa, stumble, and . . . *splat!* I fall right into the cement.

Bree comes back with the glitter to find me still sitting in the cement.

"Nancy, what happened?" Bree asks.

"I can forget about being memorable," I tell her. "I have to tell Dad I ruined his big surprise for Mom. He's going to be devastated!" That's fancy for very disappointed . . . in me.

Dad and JoJo come back outside. Dad sees the mess. He sees me too.

"Nancy, honey, it's okay," he says. "Maybe we can fix this up before the cement dries and Mom gets home."

"We . . . can?" I ask.

"We just need some new cement," Dad says.

We will have to hurry! We stir the new cement. Dad spreads it across the walkway. JoJo keeps Frenchy on the lawn.

"See, Nancy? Nothing a little elbow grease can't fix," says Dad.

"What a relief!" I say.

"Line up, everyone!" Dad says.

"Yay!" shouts JoJo as we all kneel down in front of the wet cement.

"Hands out and go!" Dad says.

Bree, JoJo, and I each put our hands in the cement.

"Footprints too," Dad adds.

As I step onto the cement, I hear a car in the driveway.

Mom is home!

"You fixed the Grand Canyon!"
Mom says. "And look at your handprints!"

Mom tries to give me a big
hug. But I'm stuck!

"Save me!" I say.

"Okay, everybody. Pretend that
it's Thanksgiving: grab an arm or a
leg!" says Dad. Everyone pulls me free!

I look down at the walkway.

"I ruined my footprints!" I say. The footprints are a funny shape, and now the cement is too dry to start over.

But Mom shakes her head.

"Nothing is ruined," Mom says. "Every time I look at this, I'll think of how much I love all of you!"

I sprinkle glitter on all of our prints. Ooh La La! Our prints sparkle in the sunlight.

"Your footprints look like butterflies!" JoJo says. She puts her arms out and starts flapping them like the wings of a butterfly.

"Or pretty fans," says Mom.

"Or the shapes your wipers make on the windshield when it's raining," says Dad.

"Sorry your prints weren't perfect like you wanted, Nancy," Bree says.

"I'm not sorry!" I say. "Not anymore."

Everyone gives me confused looks. "People are talking about my prints," I say. "That means they must be memorable!"

I guess you don't have to be *parfait* to be remembered forever.

School de Fancy

Bree and I are having a lemonade tasting today. When Bree notices our friends don't really get it, I have a fantastic idea!

"Maybe they could learn to be fancy if someone taught them how," I say. "Someone who's practically an expert in fanciness. Someone like . . . Moi."

"Congratulations," I tell Rhonda, Wanda, and Lionel. "I am going to teach you all how to be fancy!"

"I don't think I want to be fancy," says Rhonda.

"Of course you do," I say. "Being fancy makes you feel happy. Now meet me at the School de Fancy in one hour!"

"The where?" asks Lionel.

"My playhouse!" I say.

"Bonjour, class, and welcome to the School de Fancy!" I say.
Bree and I are excited to teach our friends how to be fancy.
They don't seem as excited as we are. But I continue with my
speech anyway.

"Today," I say, "we will learn three important parts of being
fancy: how to walk fancy, dress fancy, and dine fancy!"

Bree joins in. "Then you get to show what you learned in a ceremony de fancy!"

I begin with walking fancy. I place a banana on my head and show off my fancy walk. I stand up straight so the banana doesn't fall.

"Double ooh la la!" says Bree. "The banana stays on her head."

It is time for my friends to try.

"Remember, good posture," I say as I put the banana on Lionel's head. "Don't let the banana fall!"

Bree and I watch as the bananas fall. Wanda even accidentally squishes her banana!

"I think walking fancy is too hard for them," says Bree.

Dressing fancy is next! It's all about the right accessories. But my friends don't seem to like the berets, boas, and bow ties I share.

Rhonda's beret falls down over her eyes, Wanda's boa makes her sneeze, and Lionel's bow tie gets stuck on his shirt.

"I think dressing fancy is too hard for them," says Bree.

"Let's move on," I say. "Now that we know the basics, we can learn to properly dine." That's fancy for eat!

I have laid out a big basket of grapes, a small bowl of fruit, and a pitcher of lemonade. It is the perfect setting for me to show my friends how to have fancy table manners.

"Dinner is served," I say in my fanciest voice.

"I'll race ya!" Wanda says.

Lionel, Rhonda, and Wanda make a mad dash for the table.

"Wait!" I cry. "Running is not fancy!"

My friends take all the grapes and start eating them. They don't even put a napkin in their lap!

I look at Bree. "At this rate, they'll never be ready to receive their certificates de fancy!"

I need to show everyone how to serve and eat grapes properly. "It's always fancier to eat with **utensils** than with your hands," I say. Utensils are fancy for a fork, knife, and spoon. "Cut first, and then eat."

Lionel thinks he's being funny when a grape shoots off his plate.

"And no making jokes with your food!" I say.

"That's it!" says Lionel. "I'm done being fancy!"

"Yeah," Rhonda and Wanda agree. "Fancy schmancy!"

They can't give up. We still have a lot of work to do before they can receive their certificates de fancy!

"Class, I promise being fancy makes you happy," I say.

"No," Lionel says. "It makes you happy, Nancy. It's making us miserable."

"Well, if that's the way you feel, then the ceremony de fancy is canceled! Au revoir!" I say. That's French for goodbye.

As I walk away, I see Mom come outside with my glittery certificates de fancy.

"Nancy made these for you," I hear Mom tell my friends as she sets the certificates down on the table.

They are surprised. "Wow, Nancy made these for us?" Wanda asks.

"That was so nice of her," Rhonda says.

My friends decide they want to do something nice for me. Lionel
hurries over to the playhouse and yells inside.

"Oh teacher!" he says. "Your students have a surprise for you!"

I peek my head out from behind my butterfly door. "Fine, I'll go,"
I say. "But only because it is rude to refuse an invitation."

"Now the fancy ceremony thing can begin," Lionel says as I arrive.

My friends put on a show that makes them happy! First Rhonda scores with a paper ball.

Then Wanda flings her beret with a spin.

Finally, Lionel shows off his silly grape teeth.

"Even though our friends aren't fancy, they look so happy," I tell Bree.

For the grand finale, Lionel, Rhonda, and Wanda balance
bananas on their heads! I laugh and clap. "Bravo! Gold stars for
everyone," I say.

Bree and I smile at our friends. "We see that everyone has their
own way of being fancy," I say. "And as long as it makes you happy,
we think it's Magnifique!"

Nancy's Ghostly Halloween

It's Halloween! I can't wait for everyone to see my butterfly costume. It's **sublime!** That's a fancy word for really beautiful.

Bree and I are going trick-or-treating with my little sister, JoJo. She's going dressed as a knight, and it's hard to understand anything she says because her helmet is covering her face. All I hear is "Mmph, mmum, mwaa."

It's a cold day, so Mom wants me to wear a coat when we go trick-or-treating.

"Mais non, Mom!" I protest. "A coat would cover my costume."

I know, I'll wear my cloak instead. It swirls and sways to show my fabulous costume.

"Have fun, girls," Mom says. "Nancy, remember to keep an eye on your sister!"

"Wait for me!" shouts JoJo, lagging behind.

We're not too far from home when JoJo screams!

"**Sacrebleu!** Oh no, JoJo! What's the matter?" I ask.

"Those ghosts are scary!" she says, pointing to the ghost decorations in the trees.

"Don't worry," I tell JoJo. "I know those ghosts look real, but they're not."

"A-are you sure?" asks JoJo.

"**Oui**," I say. "I'm practically an expert on Halloween. You can't **let your imagination run away with you.**" That's fancy for thinking something's real when it's not.

"Come on, let's go to Mrs. Devine's," I say.

We ring Mrs. Devine's doorbell, and she opens her front door dressed as a fortune-teller.

"Bree, what a cute bunny you are," Mrs. Devine says. "And you are a very noble knight, JoJo. And, Nancy, you are one terrific . . . flying grape?"

"No," I say, "I'm a **très** fancy butterfly!"

"Of course," Mrs. Devine says. "Silly me."

As we leave, I whisk off my cloak. I'd rather be a cold butterfly than a flying grape.

"You dropped your cloak!" JoJo says behind me.

Bree and I hurry ahead to the next house. But JoJo isn't with us.

"JoJo?" I shout.

We turn back to look for her, but all we see is . . . a ghost!

"Ahhh!" we yell.

"Naaancy! Breeeee!" the ghost shouts.

"That is not a decoration," I tell Bree. "That ghost knows our names. It's real!"

Bree and I are more than scared. We are petrified! We must escape the ghost and find JoJo!

"Come back!" the ghost shouts.

Bree and I run and hide. The ghost squeaks and creaks as it chases us! When we turn and flee again, we run straight into a zombie!

"Ahhh!" we scream.

"Relax, guys," says our friend Lionel, lifting his zombie mask. "It's me. I knew my zombie costume was good, but I didn't know it was that good!"

"You don't understand, Lionel," I tell him. "We lost JoJo! And there's a real ghost chasing us!"

"Ghosts aren't real," says Lionel.

"It's true!" says Bree. "The ghost makes scary squeaks and walks spooky."

Then the ghost calls, "Liooonel!"

"It *is* real!" Lionel says. "Run!"

We run to my house to see if JoJo is there.

It's also a good place to hide from the ghost. I sincerely hope JoJo is safe inside.

We hurry into the house and close the door.

"JoJo? Are you home?" I shout. But suddenly the doorknob rattles.

"Let me in!" the ghost shouts.

We jump back in fright. There's not a word fancy enough to describe how scared I feel!

"Nancy!" I hear JoJo shout from outside.

"JoJo!" I say. I am so happy to hear my sister's voice!

But she is outside with the ghost. I must save her! I fling open the door, but I don't see the ghost.

Instead, I see JoJo sitting on the front porch wearing my cloak. I'm **puzzled,** which is fancy for confused!

"Were you wearing my cloak this whole time?" I ask JoJo.

"Mmm-hmm. But you kept running away from me," JoJo explains.
"I was just trying to give it back to you."

"Oh JoJo, we thought you were a ghost chasing us!" I say. Bree,
Lionel, and I feel silly.

"Can we go trick-or-treating now?" asks JoJo. "I want some more candy."

"Mais oui, of course!" I say. "But I should probably wear my cloak from now on."

Our night of fun is just beginning! And this time, without any ghosts chasing us. Happy Halloween!

Toodle-oo, Miss Moo

My family is having a yard sale. We're selling things we no longer need or want. We're not making a lot of money, but we're having a lot of fun!

Dad likes to make deals, and Mom is happy that we're cleaning out the house.

I've set up my own spot at the yard sale that's like a fashion **boutique**. That's French for a fancy store.

"Nancy, is there anything in here you want to keep?" Mom asks as she sets down a box of old things.

"These are baby things," I tell her. "Why would I want to keep them?"

My little sister, JoJo, asks why I'm selling things. I tell her it's a part of growing up.

Then I see Miss Moo the Zookeeper in a box of stuff.

"It's been forever since I've seen you, Miss Moo," I say. "Remember when we first met?"

I got her for my third birthday. It rained the whole time, and my cake was lopsided. But Miss Moo made everything better.

I hug Miss Moo tightly. She is just a baby toy, but I still adore her! Miss Moo was my favorite. She makes different animal noises when you push her buttons.

Suddenly, I hear Bree and her little brother, Freddy, talking about
Miss Moo.

"You don't think it's too baby-ish for you?" Bree asks.

"Nuh-huh," Freddy says. "I really, really want it."

But I don't want to sell Miss Moo. I want to keep her forever!

"Miss Moo is not my best toy for sale," I tell Freddy. "It's worn and dirty and banged-up, see? Why don't you and Bree go browse?" That's fancy for look around.

"Sorry," I whisper to Miss Moo. "I only said those things because I can't bear the thought of giving you up."

I go inside and try to hide Miss
Moo under the couch, so nobody
can buy her. I really want to keep
her. But our dog Frenchy finds her.
When Dad sees Frenchy with Miss
Moo, he picks her up and carries
her back to the yard sale.

Freddy sees Miss Moo back out on a table at the yard sale.

"There it is!" he says to Bree. "I still want it. Can I have it, Bree? Pleeeease?"

Freddy runs home to get his mom so she can buy Miss Moo for him.

Bree decides to buy Miss Moo from Dad instead, so she can surprise Freddy for his birthday. Bree comes up to me holding my old toy.

"Look what I got Freddy," Bree says. "He is going to love it."

I'm more than sad, I'm devastated. I must get Miss Moo back!

Bree leaves to walk back home, but I rush to catch up with her.

"Wait!" I shout. "May I have Miss Moo back, s'il vous plaît?" That's French for please.

"But why?" Bree asks me.

I don't know what to say, so I tell Bree I've already promised Miss Moo to a mystery customer.

"Um, I can't say who," I tell her, "but it's someone who loves Miss Moo almost as much as she loves Paris!"

Bree smiles at me. "The mystery customer is you, right?" she says.

"How did you guess?" I ask.

"Don't feel bad," she says, holding Miss Moo toward me.
"I still have baby toys too."

"No one understands me the way you do," I tell Bree, feeling relieved.

I'm so lucky to have Bree as a friend. I start to sing our friendship chant.

"Best friends, you and me," I say. Bree and I hold hands with each other.

"Better friends there could not be," we say at the same time, smiling.

We walk back to the yard sale together. I'm so happy I have Miss Moo back.

"Come on," I say to Bree. "I'll give you your money back."

"Thanks, because now I have to find Freddy another birthday present," Bree says. "It's his third birthday."

"Three?" I say, remembering my third birthday. "That's how old I was when I got . . . Miss Moo!"

I give Miss Moo to Bree.

"Birthdays are important when you are three," I say. "Freddy needs Miss Moo."

"You sure, Nancy?" Bree asks.

"Now that I'm older, I'm happier playing with more grown-up toys like Marabelle," I say.

We give Miss Moo to Freddy.

"Happy early birthday, Freddy," Bree says. "From me and Nancy."

Freddy is really happy! Freddy and Bree's mom is happy too.

"Freddy, what do you say to Bree and Nancy?"

"Thank you, thank you, thank you!" he says to us.

"It's my pleasure, Freddy," I say. "Toodle-oo, Miss Moo!"

Nancy Goes to Work

Ooh *la la!* I'm so excited! Dad usually goes to his office for work. But today he's working from home.

"Daddy, that means we can play together all day!" I say. "First, we will finish building my Eiffel Tower, then we'll make crepes, then we'll have a tickle fight and I'll win!"

Dad tells me that even though he's staying home, he still has to work.

"I promise we'll play later," he says.

I'm sad that Dad can't play with me. But suddenly I have an idea. Just because Dad has to work doesn't mean I can't spend time with him.

"If you have to work, then I will be your assistant!" I say. That's a fancy word for helper. And I'm practically an expert at helping.

First, I find an outfit in my closet that's très chic! That's French for very stylish. Then I help Dad find a quiet place to work. Voilà! My playhouse will make the perfect office! It even has a desk.

"This will do just fine," Dad says. "Thank you very much, assistant."

I set up my own desk outside of the playhouse.

"What can I assist you with now, boss?" I ask. Boss is fancy for the person in charge.

"Can you seal these envelopes and put stamps on them, please?" Dad asks. "I need to mail them today."

"Oui!" I say.

My little sister, JoJo, wants to help. I promote JoJo from little sister to assistant to the assistant. A promotion is fancy for moving up to a more important job.

"Now lick these envelopes!" I say. "And I'll stamp them."

But Dad's stamps are too plain. JoJo and I go inside to get fancier stamps.

120

JoJo and I start stamping. The envelopes look *fantastique!* That's French for fantastic.

"This is fun!" JoJo says.

"Work is fun," I say. "But to make the boss happy, we need to make these letters even fancier. I know! Let's add glitter!"

"And sparkles!" JoJo says.

"Now let's do something nice and helpful," I tell JoJo. "We will mail these for Dad."

JoJo and I run to the mailbox. JoJo smiles. "I wanna help the boss!" she says.

I stuff the letters into the mailbox. I am almost one hundred percent positive the boss will love how helpful I am!

JoJo and I can't wait to tell Dad what a great job we did.

"We stamped the envelopes and mailed them," I tell him.

"We used fancy stamps like these," says JoJo.

Dad looks worried. "The envelopes won't get where they need to go without those stamps on them," he says.

Sacrebleu! Oh no! I made a mistake.

Dad and I run to the mailbox on the double. That's fancy for right away. We need to get those envelopes, or they won't go to the right place. But the mailman has already taken the envelopes!

"Oh Dad!" I cry. "I feel terrible, awful, worse than bad! I didn't know my fancy stamps weren't the kind for mail."

"It's okay, Nancy," Dad says. "I'm not mad."

Then I see the mailman's truck.

"Dad!" I say. "Dad, look!"

But Dad is on the phone with his boss. I need to get those envelopes before Dad tells his boss what happened. That would be a disaster!

"Attendez!" I shout toward the mailman. That's French for wait.

The mailman gives me back the envelopes. I'm more than happy,
I'm ecstatic!

"Dad! I have the envelopes," I shout. "The mailman was parked
behind that tree!"

"All right! My assistant saved the day!" Dad says.

I tell Dad I'm sorry. He knows I was only trying to help.

Together, Dad and I put the right stamps on the envelopes. JoJo helps too. The envelopes still look fancy but now they will go to the right place.

"Good work, assistant," Dad says. "And great work, assistant to the assistant."

"Merci beaucoup!" I say. That's French for thank you very much.

"All done!" JoJo says as we put the last stamp on the last envelope.

"I'm glad the job is finally done," Dad says. "Now it's officially playtime!"

Dad chases me and JoJo. We all laugh. Being an assistant is hard but working with my dad and JoJo makes it fun.

"Yay!" I say. "Now you can finally help me build my Eiffel Tower!"

"Anything you say, boss," Dad says.

Shoe La La!

What a magnificent day for a stroll down the boulevard. That's a fancy word for street. Mom and I are in town doing some shopping. As we walk, I like to look in the store windows.

"Come on, Nancy," Mom says. "Keep up!"

"But how can I keep up when we are passing so many fabulous stores!" I say.

When we pass the shoe store, I see something so fancy, it makes me stop in my tracks. "Double, triple, quadruple ooh la la!" I say. "Those shoes are more than beautiful! They're exquisite!"

I ask Mom if we can go inside the store, so I may try on the shoes. Mr. Chen, the store clerk, helps me slip them on my feet.

"These beauties just came in yesterday," Mr. Chen says. "How do they feel?"

"They feel like . . . destiny," I say. That's fancy for these shoes and I were meant for each other.

"Oh my dear darling shoes," I say. "Imagine how sublime our life will be together."

The shoes are fancier than I even imagined.

I dream about what it would be like to wear these exquisite shoes as I stroll through the streets of Paris. Everyone stops what they're doing to look at my fancy shoes.

Mom asks how much the shoes cost and seems a little surprised by the answer.

"I'm sorry, sweetie," Mom says to me. "That's too much for shoes you can't wear every day."

"But . . ." I say.

"Sorry, Nancy. The answer is no," Mom says.

Mom and I go home, and I have no more joie de vivre. That's French for joyful love of life.

Just when I'm certain things can't get any worse, I see Grace riding her bike . . . wearing my red shoes!

"Hi, Nancy," she says. "Like my new shoes?"

I run home and tell Mom.

"I know it's hard seeing your friend with something you want," Mom says. But she still says no to buying the shoes.

Suddenly, I have an idea. Maybe Dad will buy me the shoes! When I tell him about them, Mom overhears me and tells him the shoes are forty dollars.

"Sorry, Nancy," Dad says. "My answer is the same as Mom's."

Then I remember I have money saved up in my piggy bank. I can use it to get the shoes! I quickly run to my room and open a drawer.

I am saving to buy something fancy, and nothing is fancier than the red shoes. I can practically feel them on my feet now.

I carry the piggy bank to my bed and count every cent. I only have twenty dollars. It's not enough!

At lunch, I tell everyone the horrible news. Mom says I can earn
the rest of the money I need by doing extra chores around the house.
Working to earn money? I never thought of that before! I love this
idea. I run to go clean my room.

Cleaning my room takes a lot of work.
When I'm finished, I lead Mom up to my
room to show her how good it looks.

Mom likes my tidy room but thinks
that keeping it clean is already my job.

Mom and Dad give me a list of other
jobs, but they are très difficile. That's
French for very difficult.

I start by working in Mom's garden. She gives me five dollars to pull a few weeds! Then I walk Mrs. Devine's dog, Jewel. Next, I help Dad paint the fence in our yard, and sweep the porch for Bree's mom. It's a long day, but I finally have forty dollars! Fantastique! That's French for fantastic.

Mom and I go to the shoe store.

"Bonjour!" I say to Mr. Chen in my fanciest voice. "One pair of sublime red shoes in size ten!"

"I was hoping to see you back," says Mr. Chen as he rings up my shoes on the cash register.

Sacrebleu! That's French for oh no! I need three more dollars for sales tax.

I'm disappointed. I thought I had enough money for the fancy shoes. But then I realize I can just work a little harder and get the rest of the money. It will be okay!

When I turn to leave, I see a lady trying on high heels. They are a beautiful Violet color! That's fancy for purple. But the lady looks unsure.

So I walk up to her.

"I'm practically an expert on shoes," I say. "Those shoes will fancy up any outfit. You should get them."

The lady smiles and thanks me. She is grateful for my advice
and decides to buy the shoes.

"Here's a tip for your fashion stylist services," she says, handing
me money.

The lady gives me three dollars! That's enough to finally buy
the shoes.

"Merci beaucoup!" I say. That's French for thanks a lot!

"I hope you enjoy your new shoes," she says.

I tell her I am almost one hundred percent certain I will. All that hard work was worth it! Ooh la la! My fancy red shoes and I are together at last!

The Case of the Disappearing Doll

I'm hosting a fancy tea party in my room. While I set the table for my guests, Mom is changing my bed.

"I have no idea how you find anything in here, Nancy," Mom says, looking around my room.

"Don't worry," I tell her. "It's organized chaos." That's fancy for I know exactly where everything is.

Bree and her doll Chiffon arrive for our party.

"Bonjour, hello," I greet them. But when I go to get my doll Marabelle, her doll bed is empty!

"Marabelle must be in her dressing room," I tell Bree. "She loves looking fancy for tea parties. Or she may be in her vacation chateau." That's French for house.

I look all around my room, but I can't find Marabelle anywhere!

"You probably just put her someplace weird and forgot," says Bree.

"Bree, Marabelle is my most beloved doll in the world. I would never forget where I put her," I say.

"Well, she couldn't have disappeared into thin air!" says Bree.

"If Marabelle is missing, it can only mean one thing," I say. "Someone took her!"

This is more than terrible. It's heartbreaking!

"But why would someone take Marabelle?" asks Bree.

Those are exactly the kinds of questions we need to be asking. Why? And who?

"It's a mystery!" I say. "We've got to solve the Case of the Disappearing Doll."

"What's the plan?" asks Bree.

"The plan?" I say. "Find Marabelle, so this hole in my heart can heal and I can live again. That's the plan!"

"What do we do first?" asks Bree. "Look for clues?"

"First we must look . . . like sleuths," I say. That's fancy for people who solve mysteries. We put on our sleuth outfits.

"Let's go to headquarters," I say.

"Where?" asks Bree.

"My playhouse!" I say.

I sigh as I look out the playhouse window to where JoJo and Freddy are playing in the yard.

"You know, maybe JoJo took Marabelle. She's always taking my things. Let's **interview** her!" I say. That's fancy for asking lots and lots of questions.

"Where were you today?" I ask JoJo. "Did you take something that isn't yours?"

"I took your popcorn!" she admits. "Mommy left it for you, but I ate it. I'm sorry!"

"Not popcorn," I say. "I meant Marabelle."

"Oh, I didn't take her," JoJo says.

"Okay, fine," I say. "But if you didn't take Marabelle, then who did?"

Just then, we see Grace ride by on her bike.

"Is that a doll in Grace's basket?" asks Bree.

We try to look closer, but we can't
see if it's Marabelle.

"What are you guys doing?"
Grace asks as she parks her bike.

I reach into Grace's bicycle basket
and pull out a doll.

"Gotcha!" I shout.

"Nancy, why would I want your doll?" asks Grace. "My doll Penelope was made specially to look like me. We even have the same outfit."

"Mais oui, of course," I say. "I was just making sure you had the right doll, and since you do . . . uh, au revoir." That's French for goodbye.

Bree and I go back to my room. I see a new clue on the floor.

"It's just a hair tie," says Bree.

"It's tan," I say. "Tan is ordinary." That's fancy for plain.

"And you would never wear anything ordinary. Wait, you're not thinking . . ." Bree gasps.

"Mom took Marabelle!" I say. "This is Mom's hair tie."

"But why would your mom take Marabelle?" asks Bree.

"I spend a lot of time with her," I say. "Maybe Mom is jealous!"

We hear noises in the basement.

"Mom's down there," I say. "Come on! Time is of the essence."

That's fancy for time is running out.

We see Mom's shadow behind a big white sheet holding what looks like my doll.

"A-ha!" I shout, holding up the hair tie. "Recognize this, Mom?"

"Oh thanks. It must have fallen out when I was in your room," says Mom.

"When you were in there taking Marabelle?" I ask.

"No, when I was in there getting your sheets for laundry," says Mom.

"Sweetie, do you really think I'd take your doll?" Mom asks.

"Well, if you didn't take her, where is she?" I say. "We can't find her anywhere!"

"Where did you last see her?" asks Mom.

"Yeah, let's retrace your steps," says Bree.

Today was like any other day . . . I got Marabelle out of bed, changed her for the tea party, then put her on my bed . . .

"My bed!" I shout.

"Maybe Marabelle is in the sheets!" I say.

We look through Mom's laundry basket, but she's not in there.

The washing machine clicks as it starts to fill with water. When I turn to look, I see Marabelle inside!

Mom stops the washer and opens the door so we can rescue Marabelle.

I am so happy to see my doll! I look over at Mom and smile.

"I'm sorry," I say. "I shouldn't have blamed you for taking Marabelle."

Mom understands and accepts my apology.

"Next time something's missing, I'm going to retrace my steps first," I say. "I blamed JoJo, Grace, and Mom for taking Marabelle before I knew for sure."

"Oh Bree," I say. "All that time I was looking for the person guilty of taking Marabelle. Yet truth be told, I was the guilty one."

"Don't be so hard on yourself," says Bree. "You're a great sleuth! Now, can we please have our tea party?"

"Oui, yes!" I say.

The Case of the Disappearing Doll is officially closed!

Mademoiselle Mom

Oh no! Mom has a wretched cold. That's fancy for awful.

"Achoo!" She sneezes and sits down in her seat. Then she blows her nose.

My little sister, JoJo, doesn't notice that Mom is sick. She just wants to play pirate.

"Mommy, watch this!" says JoJo, spinning around.

"Those sniffles sound awful," I say. "You need to go to your room and rest, Mademoiselle!" That's French for young lady.

"Oh, that's sweet of you, Nancy," Mom says. "But there's just too much to do."

"Whenever I'm not feeling well, you always tell me to rest," I say.

"But what about you and JoJo?" Mom asks.

"I can help," I tell Mom. "I can watch JoJo. I'm practically an expert at being a big sister."

"I could use a nap," says Mom.

"Don't worry," I say. "I have everything under control."

"Okay, Nancy," says Mom. "You're in charge. I'll be in my room if you need me, and Dad will be home soon."

"I'm in charge?" I say. "I'm Mom for the day!"

I imagine what that will be like. The kitchen will be spotless. I'll make a delicious dinner. Everything in the house will be *parfait!* That's French for perfect!

Suddenly JoJo tugs on my shirt. "I'm hungry," she says. "I want PB and J."

"Since I'm in charge, I'll make you a snack!" I say.

I look around. The kitchen is messy. The towels need folding. But JoJo's snack comes first. I open the pantry and get out the peanut butter and jelly.

"One sandwich coming right up," I tell her.

I start to make a PB and J, and JoJo takes a juice box.

"Put the straw in," she says.

"Say 'please,'" I tell her in my best Mom voice. "Or s'il vous plaît if you want to speak French."

The straw goes in, and a big squirt comes out!

"Oops, sorry," says JoJo.

I know it was an accident, so I can't be mad.

"I miss Mommy!" JoJo says.

She runs to the stairs. But I stop her just in time.

"If you wake Mommy, we can't play my fun game," I say. "It's called folding towels!"

But JoJo wants to play pirate. She hops into the laundry basket. I grab all the clean towels.

"Whoa!" says JoJo. "A wave!"

When I put the clean towels on the kitchen table, I see JoJo's untouched sandwich.

"Are you going to eat your snack, JoJo?" I ask. She is too busy playing pirate to answer.

I go to wrap it up for later. But Frenchy gets there first!

Then it gets very quiet. I see JoJo trying to sneak upstairs.

"JoJo, wait!" I say. "Mom's resting."

"But I miss Mommy!" she says. "You're not playing the way Mommy does."

Sacrebleu! Oh no! JoJo is going to wake up Mom!

How does Mom do it all?
I know! She always does more
than one thing at a time. I try it!
First, I spin JoJo.

Then I fold the towels.

I push JoJo across the floor.

I wipe the counter.

Next, I load the dishwasher and add the dishwashing soap.

"The more soap," I say, "the cleaner the dishes will be."

When Mom sees all the work I've done, she's going to be happy, thrilled, elated!

Oh no! Hundreds of bubbles come pouring out of the dishwasher!
This is more than bad—it is terrible!
"I need Mom!" I say.

I run upstairs, but Mom is asleep. I can't disturb poor sniffly Mom. But I don't know what to do. There are bubbles everywhere and I was only trying to help!

But I realize Mom would fix it all somehow. But since I'm in charge, I guess it's up to Moi! That's French for me.

When I come back to the kitchen, JoJo is playing in the bubbles.
I start mopping up the mess with the clean towels I just folded.

Finally, Dad comes home.

"Don't worry, Dad," I tell him. "Mom left me in charge."

"Um, and it looks like you're doing a good job, Nancy. Maybe I should help," he says.

"Merci, Dad," I say. "If you insist!"

We work together and soon the bubbles are all cleaned up. When Mom comes downstairs after her nap, the kitchen is sparkling.

"What happened in here? It looks like the whole room took a bath," she says.

"I don't know how you do it, Mom," I tell her. "Taking care of the house, JoJo, Frenchy, the dishes, and laundry is more than tiring, it's exhausting!"

I think I'll let Mom be in charge again. And I'll go back to being Moi!

Ice Skater Extraordinaire

I'm *très* excited because my best friend, Bree, is coming ice skating with us today.

"Can you believe I've only ever been ice skating in my living room?" I ask Bree. "If I'm this good at skating in my socks, I'm going to be amazing with ice skates on. I'll be an ice skater *extraordinaire!*" That's French for extraordinary.

When we get to the rink, Bree tells me that even though she's taken lessons, she can't do any fancy moves yet.

"Don't worry," I tell Bree. "The only thing that matters is that we're best friends skating together."

We put on our ice skates. Bree has her own skates, but my rental skates look old. Bree and I use our hair accessories to fancy them up. Voilà!

We head out onto the ice. Time to be extraordinary! But I keep falling down. I am baffled. That's fancy for confused.

"Maybe it's because it's your first time skating on ice," says Bree.

But I know that can't be the case. I'm almost one hundred percent positive my skates are broken. I'll ask Mom to get me new ones.

Mom tells me I don't need new skates. She says I need to practice.
Mom tells me I should use a walker. "It'll help you stay balanced."

"No way!" I protest. "Walkers are for little kids like JoJo! An
expert would never use such a thing."

"I bet an expert might . . . if they were a beginner," Mom says.

"If I use a walker, I'll look absurd!" I say. That's fancy for foolish.

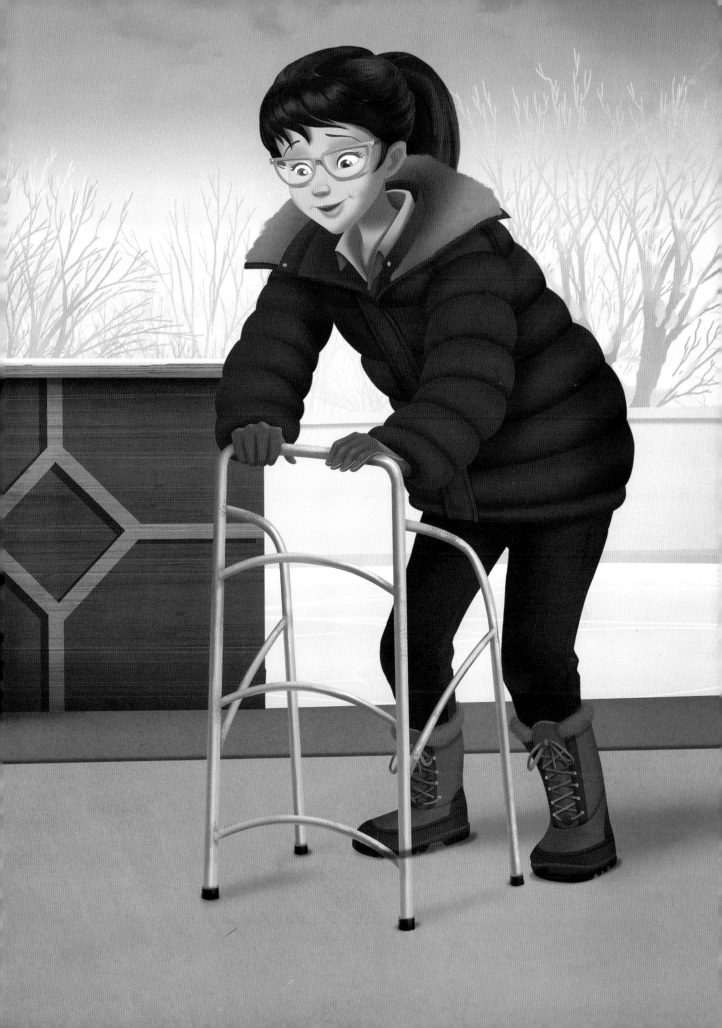

"Nancy, did you get new skates?" Bree asks.

I tell Bree I have bad, awful, terrible news. Mom says I need to practice with a walker!

"So? I used a walker when I started skating too," says Bree.

"If I can't be extraordinary, then I just won't skate!" I say.

"But you said that skating together with me, your best friend, was all that mattered," says Bree.

"That was back when I was an expert," I tell her.

"Fine," says Bree. "I'll go skate by myself."

"Fine!" I say. "Au revoir! That's French for goodbye."

I am upset that Bree does not understand.

Then I see two friends skating together. They look so happy.

"Wait!" I shout to Bree. "I'm sorry. I want to skate together even if I'm not extraordinary. Can we try again?"

"Of course," says Bree. "I can teach you how to skate."

"Magnifique!" I say. That's French for magnificent.

But there's just one thing we need to do first.

Bree and I fancy up the walker. We use ribbons, feathers, and necklaces.

"Ooh La La, now this is something I can use!" I tell Bree.

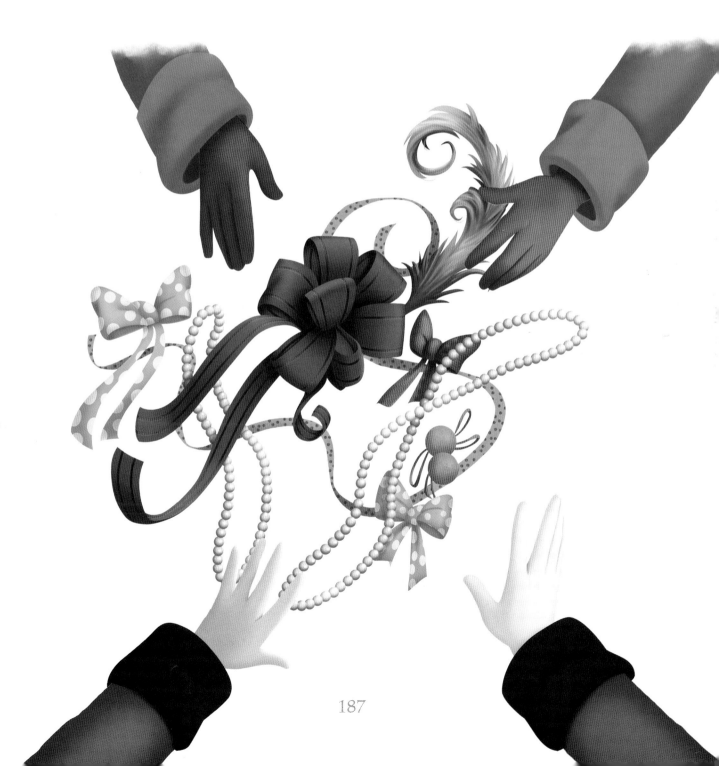

We head onto the ice. Bree gives me tips.

"Just hold on and go slow," she says.

I do just what Bree says. Even though my feet are a little wobbly, I move slowly across the ice.

"Try to glide more than step," she says. "And don't look down. Look where you're going."

"Like this?" I ask as I glide on my skates.

Bree is ecstatic! That's fancy for very happy. "You're doing it!" she says.

"Merci!" I say. That's French for thank you. "I'll be an expert in no time."

I practice and practice and soon I improve! I don't even fall down!

"Want to go around again?" Bree asks.

"Oui! Yes!" I say. "Let's go around a hundred times!"

I see Mom, Dad, and JoJo watching us.

"Look!" JoJo says. She takes a drawing of flowers from her coloring book. "Yay! Flowers for Nancy!" she says.

Maybe one day I'll be an ice skater extraordinaire. But for now, it's extraordinary to be ice skating with my best friend.

Fancy Nancy's
FANCY & FRENCH Words

These are the fancy words in this book:

Absolument: French for absolutely

Absurd: foolish

Assistant: helper

Attendez: French for wait

Au revoir: French for goodbye

Baffled: confused

Bon appétit: French for enjoy your meal

Bonjour: French for hello

Boss: person in charge

Boulevard: street

Boutique: French for a fancy store

Browse: look around

Chandelier: hanging light

Chateau: French for house

Chez: French for house of

Destiny: something is meant to be

Devastated: very disappointed

Dine: to eat

Ecstatic: more than happy

Exhausting: more than tiring

Extraordinaire: French for extraordinary

Fantastique: French for fantastic

Fiasco: everything has gone wrong

Heartbreaking: more than terrible

Indisposed: someone can't make it

Interview: to ask lots of questions

Jeté: French for leap

Joie de vivre: French for joyful love of life

Lavish: fancy

Let your imagination run away with you: thinking something's real when it's not

Mademoiselle: French for young lady

Magnifique: French for magnificent

Mais non: French for but no

Mais oui: French for of course

Memorable: being famous forever

Merci beaucoup: French for thank you very much

Merci: French for thank you

Mesmerized: when you can't take your eyes off something

Moi: French for me

Obedient: your pet does what you say

On the double: right away

Ooh la la: French for wow

Ordinary: plain

Organized chaos: to know where everything is

Oui: French for yes

Papillon: French for butterfly

Parfait: French for perfect

Petrified: more than scared

Pizzazz: style

Promote: moving up to a more important job

Puzzled: confused

S'il vous plaît: French for please

Sacrebleu: French for oh no

Sleuths: people who solve mysteries

Spectacular: amazing

Sublime: really beautiful

Time is of the essence: time is running out

Toast: fancy thing people do when they want to say something nice about someone

Très: French for very

Très chic: French for very stylish

Très difficile: French for very hard

Très elegant: French for very elegant

Utensils: a fork, knife, and spoon

Violet: purple

Voilà: French for look at that!

Wretched: awful